Lulu's Holiday

To Freddie, Olive and Joe
with love

You can also read

Hello Lulu
ISBN 1 84121 143 5

and

Lulu's Busy Day
ISBN 1 84121 145 1

and

Happy Birthday Lulu
ISBN 1 84121 735 2

ORCHARD BOOKS
96 Leonard Street, London EC2A 4XD
Orchard Books Australia
Unit 31/56 O'Riordan Street, Alexandria NSW 2015
1 84121 762 X (hardback)
1 84121 088 9 (paperback)
First published in Great Britain in 2001
First paperback publication in 2002
Copyright © Caroline Uff 2001
The right of Caroline Uff to be identified as the author
and the illustrator of this work has been asserted by her in
accordance with the Copyright, Designs and Patents Act, 1988.
A CIP catalogue record for this book is available from the British Library.
10 9 8 7 6 5 4 3 2 1 (hardback)
10 9 8 7 6 5 4 3 2 1 (paperback)
Printed in Singapore

Lulu's Holiday

Caroline Uff

little ORCHARD

Hello
Lulu.

Are you going
on holiday?

Lulu packs her rucksack.

Don't forget Teddy!

Off we go. Toot toot! Clickety clack over the track.

Let's play I Spy
out of the window.

"I can see the sea!"
says Lulu.
And look, here's Lulu's
holiday house.

It's very hot.

Rub, rub, rub, on with the suncream.

Lulu plays in the sand.

"Hello, little crabs," she says.

Lulu's big sister swims
with water wings.

Splish splash!

"I like paddling best,"
says Lulu.

Hooray, picnic time!
What's inside
the hamper,
Lulu?

Lulu's puppy is hungry too.
Woof woof!

What a beautiful sandcastle, Lulu.

All decorated with shells
and stones.
"Oops, sand's not for eating!"
says Lulu.

Yum, yum, strawberry ice cream.

What a lovely picture, Lulu.
Shall we send it to Granny?

Home again,
home again.
Jiggety jig.

"Goodnight stars," says Lulu. Lulu loves being on holiday.